the Tear Thief

written by Carol Ann Duffy

illustrated by Nicoletta Ceccoli

Barefoot Books
Celebrating Art and Story

Late one evening, the Tear Thief crept into a town. The Tear
Thief was invisible and carried a silvery waterproof
sack on her back. Only if you happened to look
into a puddle as she was passing could you see what
the Tear Thief looked like because a puddle was the
one thing that showed her reflection. The Tear Thief had
short spiky white hair and big grey eyes. She
wore a handkerchief dress and silk slippers that made
no sound as she walked.

The Tear Thief came to a quiet road
with a neat row of houses and flew
into a tall tree there for a good look and
a listen. It was the hour between supper and
bedtime. All the curtained windows were flushed with light,
and enticing smells of soup and stew and pasta and onions
(the Tear Thief's favourite) and rhubarb crumble were
drifting up and away into the deepening dusk.
The Tear Thief listened hard with sharp ears.

'Boo-hoo-hoo!'

A child was crying.

The Tear Thief jumped lightly from the top of the tree on to the roof of the first house. She crept along the rooftops, silent as smoke, listening, listening, until she heard the crying again.

'Boo-hoo-hoo!'

Ha! The crying was coming from Number 17. Quick as a blink, the Tear Thief slid down the chimney into the attic and pressed her ear to a floorboard.

'Boo! Boo-hoo! Boo-hoo-hoo!'

Down the stairs, sly as steam, sneaked the Tear Thief, on to the landing and into the bathroom. A boy was sitting in the bath crying his eyes out. His mother was kneeling by the side of the bathtub holding a pink bottle of strawberry shampoo.

The Tear Thief sat perched on the edge of the bath,
watching excitedly and loosening the top of her sack.

'I don't want to be shampooooed!' wailed the boy in the bubbles.

'Stop this silly crying,' said the boy's mother, 'or the Tear
Thief will hear you.'

The boy stopped crying and stared at his mother.
A single plump tear dangled from the
end of his nose like a pearl.

The Tear Thief pounced. In one quick movement she
snatched the gleaming tear from the boy's nose
and popped it into her sack.

'Oh!' gasped the boy as his last tear
seemed to disappear into thin air.

'I told you,' said his mother. 'That was
probably the Tear Thief.'

The boy and his mother started to laugh, but by now
the Tear Thief had flown across the hall, out through
the front door and had shimmied
halfway up a lamp-post. She
sat on the top, swinging her
legs and listening.

'Waaah! Waaah! Waaah!'

Through an open upstairs window at Number 25 came
the sound of bad-tempered screaming and sobbing.
The Tear Thief slipped down the lamp-post and
slithered up a drainpipe to get to the window. Her
wide grey eyes stared in at a child's bedroom.

A red-faced girl in a nightdress was jumping
up and down having a terrible tantrum and scattering
tears all over the room like fistfuls of gravel.

'I WANT CHOCOLATE!

I WANT CHOCOLATE!' bawled the girl.

The Tear Thief hopped into the room and began to
steal the girl's tears: 5, 10, 15, 20, 25, 30 . . .
into the silvery sack they went . . . 40, 50, 60, 70 . . .
The more tears the Tear Thief collected,
the more tired the girl became until eventually she
sat down on the floor with her back against the wall
and fell fast asleep.
The Tear Thief slipped out through the window.

A light rain began to fall, orange under the street lights. The Tear Thief worked hard. She stole the oddly long tears of a boy who had trapped his finger in a flute. She stole the tiny tears of a baby having her nappy changed. Into the sack: the tears shed by a pair of twins fighting over an orange teddy bear. Into the sack: two pear-shaped tears from the sly cheeks of a boy who'd been caught telling a lie about a big hole in his trousers.

The tears were jewels inside the darkness of the sack,

clinking and chinking and winking. Tears of rage

were red and glowed like rubies.

Tears of envy or jealousy were as green as emeralds.

Tears of self-pity were turquoise.

Scared tears were white like moonstones

and guilty tears were amber.

Rain gurgled and chuckled in the gutters. Here

and there a puddle stared up from the pavement.

The Tear Thief listened, peeped, crept, climbed,

pinched, nicked, filched and purloined until her sack

was brimming with tears. She set off
down the road as the last of the
rain stopped falling. A girl was standing alone
under a lamp-post on the corner.

As the Tear Thief sneaked
past the girl, she noticed
she was quietly crying. The Tear Thief
stopped. There was always room
in the sack for a few more tears. She looked
carefully at the girl's tears. They were very special. They were
tears of real sadness. The Tear Thief could tell
that just one of these tears was worth a hundred cried
over spilt milk or a thousand crocodile tears. She reached out
her pale hand to pluck one from the girl's cheek.

Just then the girl wiped her eyes with her sleeve
and looked sadly into a puddle. The Tear
Thief's mischievous face stared up at her.

'Eeek!' squealed the girl and turned round
to look behind herself.

There was nobody there.

The girl looked at the puddle again. Sure enough,
there was the reflection of the Tear Thief in the water.

'Who are you?' asked the girl.

'I am the Tear Thief.'

The girl knelt down by the puddle and
stared hard at the Tear Thief's reflection.

'How old are you?'

'As old as joy and sorrow.'

'Where do you live?'

'In every place where children cry.'

'Were you going to steal my tears?'

'Yes,' said the face of the Tear Thief in the
puddle. 'Your tears are the most precious
tears of all. They are worth more than diamonds.'

The girl stood up again. Her face
was still wet with tears, like the
leaves of the trees were
with the rain. She gently wiped off
one of her own tears with her
fingertip and stared at it. She could see
the reflection of the Tear Thief there as well!

'But why are my tears so precious?' asked the girl.

'I will tell you everything,' said the Tear Thief,
'if you give me your tears. Just close your eyes and listen.'

So the girl closed her eyes and the Tear Thief
gathered the tears from her eyelashes and cheeks
as she whispered to her:

'Each night, in the hour between supper and bedtime,
I visit a different street and I steal the tears of every
child who cries. When my sack is full, I climb up to the moon
and I pour my sack of tears into the moon's light. The
light of the moon is made from tears of laughter or pain or anger
or boredom, from every kind of tear you can think of –
but the most beautiful part of the
moon's light comes
from tears of pure
sadness. And that is
what your tears are.'

'Yes,' said the girl.
'It's because I've
lost my little dog.'

She opened her eyes as she said this and looked again
in the puddle but there was nobody there. She ran
along the street to the next puddle and stared into it,
then the next and the next and the next.
But they were just ordinary puddles with
nothing special in them at all. The girl ran round the corner,
looking down at all the puddles as she ran. Then she ran
round another corner, and another, searching in
every puddle for one more glimpse of the
Tear Thief. But it was no use. The Tear Thief was gone.

'Woof!' The girl looked up. 'Woof! Woof!'

A little black dog with a white chest was sitting under
a tree at the end of the street.

The girl called out her dog's name. 'It's you!' she said.
'I've found you!' And so she had. Her lost dog was
splashing towards her through the puddles.

The girl was safely tucked up in bed and the dog
was safely curled up in his basket. The rain had
stopped completely now and all the puddles
were shrinking. The night was calm and quiet. The girl always
left her curtains open so that she could see
the star she was born under if she opened her eyes.

She opened them now. Outside her window a full
moon rose, huge and luminous.

'Oh!' gasped the girl.

She got out of bed and went to the window. It was the most
        beautiful moon she had ever seen in her whole young life!
Light poured from it in a million different moonbeams. The
            girl saw the light of the moon in her garden, turning
        the leaves on the trees to silver. Beyond that, she
saw the light of the moon on the rooftops of all the houses,
            like honey. A midnight cat walked along a wall and the
        light of the moon made its eyes burn gold. The whole
                town moon-bathed as it slept. The river lay on its
back and gazed up at the moon, dazzled and lovesick.

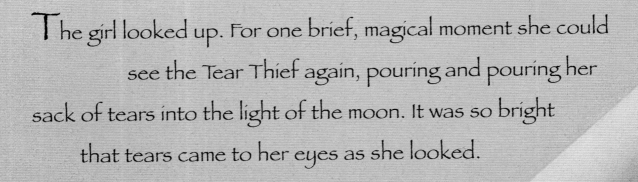

The girl looked up. For one brief, magical moment she could
see the Tear Thief again, pouring and pouring her
sack of tears into the light of the moon. It was so bright
that tears came to her eyes as she looked.

Her dog snuffled in his basket.

In the house next door, on the other
side of the wall, the newborn
baby started to cry.

For Ella with love from Mommy — C. A. D.
To Mara and the wonder in her wide eyes — N. C.

Barefoot Books · 124 Walcot Street · Bath BA1 5BG

Graphic design by Barefoot Books Ltd. Reproduction by Grafiscan, Verona

This book was typeset in Papyrus. The illustrations were prepared in acrylics on canvas

ISBN 978-1-84686-394-3

British Cataloguing-in-Publication Data:
a catalogue record for this book is available from the British Library

1 3 5 7 9 8 6 4 2